The Best Burro

OUR WORLD OF PEOPLE SERIES

Mexico

The Best Burro

© 1967 GENERAL LEARNING CORPORATION
ALL RIGHTS RESERVED
PRINTED IN THE UNITED STATES OF AMERICA
PHILIPPINES COPYRIGHT 1967 BY GENERAL LEARNING CORPORATION
PUBLISHED SIMULTANEOUSLY IN CANADA

This publication or parts thereof may not be
reproduced in any form by photographic, electrostatic,
mechanical, or any other method, for any use, including
information storage and retrieval, without written
permission from the publisher.

Library of Congress Catalog Card Number: 67-16755

By Frederick J. Moffitt

Illustrated by Don Bolognese

CONSULTANTS:

V. PHILLIPS WEAVER, Associate Professor
of Early Childhood—Elementary Education,
University of Maryland

CHRISTINE B. GILBERT, Librarian,
Plandome Road School, Manhasset, New York;
Adjunct Associate Professor of Library Science,
Graduate Library School, Long Island University

SILVER BURDETT COMPANY
A Division of General Learning Corporation
Morristown, New Jersey • Park Ridge, Ill. • Palo Alto • Dallas • Atlanta

In a little adobe home high on a hillside, a Mexican family is eating breakfast. Benito, the son, eats very quickly.

He scoops the hot, red beans with a rolled tortilla and takes a big bite. He gulps his coffee with the hot milk in it. He gobbles a fresh melon his sister Rosa just picked from the garden.

Benito doesn't have to hurry this morning because there is no school. But he hurries anyway. He wants tomorrow to come quickly.

Father finishes his breakfast and leaves the table. "Where are you going, Tata? May I come too?" Benito asks his father.

"No," says Tata. "Today you must take care of the farm. Mama and I are going to town to buy gifts for San Antonio's Day."

Benito's eyes flash. For months he has thought about San Antonio's Day. It is a very gay *fiesta*. It is a time when parents give gifts of animals to children.

The Padre blesses the animals. There is a grand parade. The animals are dressed in bows and ribbons and flowers. There is music and dancing and fireworks. There are sweet cakes to eat.

Benito can hardly wait!

"Will you buy me a *burro* for San Antonio's Day?" Benito asks.

Tata smiles. "A burro is a wonderful animal, Benito. It's strong as a horse and patient as a cow. But it can be stubborn and mean, too. I don't know of any good burros for sale right now. But we will talk about it again. Now Mama and I must go. Don't daydream. Keep your mind on the farm today."

9

"If I'm big enough to watch the farm," thinks Benito, "I can surely take care of a burro. Even an old burro could help carry sugarcane to market."

"Benito," calls Rosa, as she sweeps the adobe floor, "don't forget to fill the water jug for Mama's flowers. And when you're done, come help me in the house."

"I'll stay in the field," decides Benito. "Rosa always has something for me to do."

Every evening, he helps his sister. Benito thinks it is bad enough to mix powders for the paints Rosa uses. The pottery she paints is beautiful, but Benito feels too big to work with women.

"Let the women weave baskets and make pottery!" he says to himself. "I'd rather work in the field as a man does."

Benito weeds in the garden and dreams of a burro of his own. A burro would be such a help. It would also be his friend.

A burro might even win a prize at the San Antonio's Day parade. But Benito knows he won't get the prize tomorrow. His only pet is sleepy, lop-eared old Rabbit. Rabbit never wins prizes. All he does is run away.

Benito is thinking about San Antonio's Day when Señor Moreno comes up the hill. His scrawny little burro is with him. Her name is Isabel, and she is carrying a load of sugarcane as big as a haystack.

Señor Moreno is shouting at Isabel to hurry up. He has a loud voice and a bad temper. But Isabel has a loud voice and a bad temper, too.

Isabel is a stubborn burro. As she comes by Benito's gate, she stops and sits down.

Señor Moreno shouts. He pulls. He pushes. He prods. He puffs. He pants. He pleads. He pokes.

It's no use. Isabel simply sits. And sits. And sits.

"You're not even worth twenty *pesos*!" Señor Moreno shouts at Isabel.

"I'll pay you ten pesos for her," says Benito. He is surprised to hear his own voice. Where will he ever get ten pesos?

"Twenty pesos!" shouts Señor Moreno.

"Fifteen pesos!" says Benito. "Isabel and I can earn the money and pay you later."

"It's a bargain," replies Señor Moreno. "The good-for-nothing burro is yours for fifteen pesos!"

Señor Moreno drags the sugarcane from Isabel's back and stomps away. He doesn't even say good-by. Isabel cries "Hee-haw! Hee-haw!" She seems happy to see him go.

"You belong to me now," says Benito. He tries to scratch her ear but she turns away.

"Come, my little friend," he says, "you can trust me." He gives her a piece of sugarcane. Isabel sticks her head forward and lets Benito pat her.

Benito speaks softly to the burro. "Our barn is filled with sweet-smelling hay. It will be your home now. Come along." Isabel gets up and follows Benito to the barn.

Lop-eared Rabbit goes, too.

When Mama and Tata return that night, Benito tells about his bargain.

Tata laughs out loud. "If you teach the burro to wiggle her ears, she might earn her way as a scarecrow." Then he is serious. "You bargained for the most balky burro in all Mexico, Benito. You may be sorry. But a bargain is a bargain. You must find a way to keep your word."

Benito wishes he could say where he will get the money to pay Señor Moreno. But he decides to worry about that later. He is sure Isabel will help when the time comes.

23

Today is San Antonio's Day! Benito gets up very early. He dresses Isabel in a fiesta costume. She looks funny with a sombrero on her head.

This is a day of joy. There is gay music and happy chatter in the village. Benito wrinkles his nose as he smells the hot tortillas and red beans frying in the open air.

He is proud of Isabel and lop-eared Rabbit. They behave very well when the Padre blesses them. The Padre says Isabel is a fine burro.

Benito watches the Padre bless other animals. Then he sees that the parade is about to begin.

A boy in the crowd points to Isabel. "Let the burro lead the parade!" he says. Benito is happy that people like his animal. He remembers how stubborn and bad Isabel was yesterday. "Maybe she is good because I am good to her," he thinks.

The parade winds through the narrow streets. Benito can't stop grinning. Isabel brays and flicks her ears. She is not "good-for-nothing" now.

The parade is finally over. The judges put their heads together. They must decide who gets the prize. On San Antonio's Day a prize is given to the animal who is best behaved. A prize is also given to the child who owns the animal.

The judges whisper. They smile. They make up their minds. Isabel and Benito get the prize!

Isabel gets a big red bow. Benito gets a shiny leather wallet with ten pesos inside.

Lop-eared Rabbit doesn't win a prize, but he takes a flower to chew from Isabel's sombrero.

That night Benito rushes home and tells Mama and Tata about the prize. "Isabel is so good. She won the money to pay Señor Moreno."

Tata frowns. "But you still need five pesos. How will you get it?"

"I have a plan," says Benito. "Isabel and I
will carry vegetables and pottery to market for
the neighbors. Isabel is a careful burro and she
won't break anything."

Soon the people call Isabel the "good burro" and
Benito earns the pesos to pay Señor Moreno.

"How did you get the pesos?" asks Señor Moreno.

Benito grins. "I treat Isabel well, and she is
happy. So she works hard for me. Now I have the
best burro in Mexico."

"Hee-haw!" Isabel seems to agree.

Helpful Words

Benito (bay NEE toh), Benedict

burro (BOO rroh), a donkey

fiesta (FYEH stah), a feast; a holiday

Padre (PAH thray), a Father; a Priest

pesos (PAY sohs), Mexican money

Rosa (ROH sah), Rose

San Antonio (sah nahn TOH nyoh), Saint Anthony

Señor Moreno (say NYOHR moh RAY noh), Mister
   Moreno

sombrero (sohm BRAY roh), a hat

Tata (TAH tah), Daddy

tortilla (tohr TEE yah), a cornmeal cake

32